Praise for

A Day with a Perfect Stranger

"Brilliant. Masterful. Filled with liberating truth."

—STEPHEN ARTERBURN, best-selling author
of *Every Man's Battle,* founder and chairman
of New Life Ministries

"Don't let David Gregory's simple writing style fool you: the message shared throughout *A Day with a Perfect Stranger* is profound, and the questions he raises are life changing."

—LIZ CURTIS HIGGS, best-selling author
of *Bad Girls of the Bible*

"Fasten your seat belt for another marvelously divine encounter with the *Perfect Stranger*! Once again, Gregory masterfully demonstrates just how passionately and intimately our God loves each one of us. If you are looking for an encouraging faith encounter, the *Perfect Stranger* books are the most palatable and powerful tools of our day."

—SHANNON ETHRIDGE, best-selling author
of *Every Woman's Battle* and *Every Woman's Marriage*

"While I liked *Dinner with a Perfect Stranger* very much, I *loved A Day with a Perfect Stranger.* This book has the potential to make people think about what drives them, what keeps them from God, and what will ultimately fulfill them. In a feelings-based and satisfaction-driven society, this is an invaluable tool. People are hungering for the answers to questions Mattie gets to ask. I can't wait to hand it out to friends who do not yet know the Stranger in their midst."

—LISA TAWN BERGREN, best-selling author
of *The Begotten*

"Sometimes the simplest books can have the most profound influence, and David Gregory has done such a wonderful job capturing my imagination. Over and over as I read *A Day with a Perfect Stranger,* I kept asking myself, what would I say if I ever sipped lattes with Jesus? And at the end of the book, I realized I have that opportunity every day. He's not only listening, but he's speaking too. Anyone who enjoyed *Dinner with a Perfect Stranger* will love the sequel."

—RENE GUTTERIDGE, best-selling author
of *BOO* and *The Splitting Storm*

a Day with a
Perfect Stranger

DAVID GREGORY

WATERBROOK
PRESS

A Day with a Perfect Stranger
Published by WaterBrook Press
12265 Oracle Boulevard, Suite 200
Colorado Springs, Colorado 80921

The events and characters (except for Jesus Christ) in this book are fictional,
and any resemblance to actual events or persons is coincidental.

ISBN: 978-0-307-73018-3
ISBN: 978-0-307-44631-2 (electronic)

The Library of Congress cataloged the hardcover edition as follows:
Gregory, David, 1959–
    A day with a perfect stranger / David Gregory. — 1st ed.
        p. cm.
    ISBN 1-4000-7242-5
    1. Jesus Christ—Fiction. 2. Imaginary conversations. 3. Married women—
Fiction. I. Title.
    PS3607.R4884D39 2006
    813'.6—dc22
                                                        2006002836

Printed in the United States of America
2011—First Trade Paperback Edition

10 9 8 7 6 5 4 3 2 1

Special Sales
Most WaterBrook books are available in special quantity discounts when purchased in
bulk by corporations, organizations and special interest groups. Custom imprinting or
excerpting can also be done to fit special needs. For information, please e-mail
SpecialMarkets@WaterBrookPress.com or call 1-800-603-7051.

For Barbara,
whose soul is satisfied

My thanks to Michael Svigel and Ava Smith
for their special contributions to this book.

one

I NEVER THOUGHT I'd become the kind of woman who would be glad to leave her family. Not that I wanted to abandon them, exactly. I was just glad to get away for a few days. Or longer, in the case of one of them.

Maybe I should have been celebrating instead of escaping. That's what you do with big news, isn't it? And we had had plenty.

A few weeks earlier my husband, Nick, told me that he had met Jesus. Not the usual "getting saved" kind of meeting Jesus. I mean, met Jesus. Literally. At a local Italian restaurant.

At first I thought he was joking, of course. He wasn't. Then I thought he had been hallucinating. He had, after all, been putting in seventy-hour weeks at work and getting limited sleep. But he stuck to his story, which left me with— I didn't know what.

All I knew was that my husband was convinced he had dined with Jesus, and he had turned into some kind of Jesus freak. It was bad enough that he had previously disappeared into his work. Now when we were together, God was all he wanted to talk about. That wasn't the "till death do us part" I had planned on.

Things had been strained enough between us without bringing God into the mix. It was as if someone had kidnapped the real Nick and replaced him with a religious Nick clone. There we were, plugging along in our marriage, and suddenly Nick, who wouldn't have been caught dead in a church parking lot, is best friends with deity.

It's not that I object to religion. People can believe whatever they want to. I just didn't grow up religious, hadn't become religious, and didn't marry someone religious. And I wanted it to stay that way.

So getting away from Nick for four days was a relief. What I hated was leaving Sara, my two-year-old. Granted, I looked forward to the break, as any mother would. But I had never been away from her longer than two nights, and even then I found myself missing her by the second day. And that was with my mom coming down to take care of her. At least I trusted my mom. No telling what might happen with Nick doing the childcare. Not that he was a bad dad, when he was both home and off his cell phone.

But I had to take this trip. A client had built a resort hotel near Tucson and wanted me to design new brochures for it. The manager insisted on giving me a personal tour of the place. She said I needed to experience it firsthand to fully capture its essence. And get a free massage, I hoped.

I rarely had to travel for my graphic arts work, which was fine with me. Most of the business I had developed since we'd moved to Cincinnati was local. Sometimes I went back to Chicago on a job, but I could handle most of my old accounts online. This, however, was my biggest client—had been for six years—and I couldn't exactly say no.

The trip should have been a one-day there-and-back. Two at the max. But since you can't get a nonstop from Cincinnati to Tucson, I booked my flight through Dallas, which meant I had to take two travel days.

I could hardly imagine a less appealing way to spend two days of my life. I don't much like air travel, anyway. I'd rather just throw some stuff in the car and hit the road. In a car no one has you stand in line or searches your purse or forces you to eat dry pretzels for a snack. Nor does anyone pull you aside, have you extend your arms, and run a baton all over your body. Why do I always get singled out?

Plus, I didn't feel the best this particular morning. I knew that getting on a plane without any breakfast wasn't a brilliant idea since they don't even serve those tasteless meals anymore. But I figured I could break down and buy a snack box if I had to.

Before heading out the front door, I wrote a note and left it on the kitchen counter.

Nick,

Sara's pajamas are in the top drawer, if you don't remember. You may not, since you haven't put her to bed this year. Her toothbrush is in the left drawer in her bathroom. I left plenty of juice, oatmeal, and cereal for breakfasts. Plus she likes toast and jelly. There's a macaroni casserole she likes in the fridge and some frozen veggies. After that runs out, she likes Chick-fil-A. Don't forget story time at the library tomorrow at 10:30.

You can reach me on my cell if you need me for anything about Sara. Hope you and Jesus have a great time together.
Mattie

I drove myself to the airport. Nick had volunteered to take me, but I declined. Riding by myself was preferable to Nick telling me about his latest discovery in the Bible, which he was now reading voraciously, or listening to Christian radio, a fate worse than death. I parked and walked into the terminal. The soft music and absence of Jesus talk provided a welcome relief.

Miraculously, I made it through security without any special groping and proceeded to my gate. Once there, I sat with my carry-ons and glanced at my boarding pass. *Oh, great,* I thought. *An E seat, in the middle. Why didn't I make my reservation earlier and get a better seat? Maybe I can switch to an aisle seat near the back of the plane.*

A minute later the agent at the gate picked up her microphone and announced, "Ladies and gentlemen, our flight to Dallas is full. To expedite your departure, please make sure you stow your bags and take your seat as quickly as possible."

Fabulous.

She then started hawking two two-hundred-dollar travel vouchers for anyone willing to take a flight four hours later. No one took them. When the offer went up to three hundred dollars, I stepped forward. *Maybe they'll have an aisle seat on the next flight.*

"When would that get me into Tucson?" I asked.

The agent looked up the connecting flight. "Ten twenty-two this evening."

Nearly ten thirty. Plus taking a shuttle out to the hotel. That's after eleven.

I decided to pass; I'd be too tired the next day.

As they called first-class passengers to board, I remembered something I'd forgotten to tell Nick. I pulled out my phone and dialed his office. He answered.

"Nick, I'm at the airport."

"Hey. How's it going?"

"Look, I forgot to tell you that Laura has Sara with their son Chris until about five thirty. She's taking them swimming at the Y."

"No problem. I'm going to get home a little early and fix something for Sara and me."

"What—you mean cook something?"

"Yeah. I'm picking up stuff for spaghetti and meatballs."

"Miracles never cease. Look, I need to go—my row is boarding."

"Call me tonight?"

"I'll see, Nick. I might be pretty tired."

"Well, have a great trip. I love you."

"Yeah. Bye, Nick."

I picked up my tote bag and suitcase and got to the boarding line just as my group was being called. I walked down the ramp and waited interminably while all the people already on the plane decided where to put their stuff. By the time I got to my row, there was room overhead for my suitcase but not my tote bag. I stowed my suitcase and looked at my seating arrangement on the left. The seats on both sides of mine were already occupied. Two guys. *Great. Sandwiched for the next two and a half hours between two men. Why couldn't they have put me between two size 2 women?* The man in the aisle seat stood up to let me by. I squeezed into the middle seat, resigning myself to not having an armrest available to me on either side. Guys always hog those.

I leaned down, stuffed my bag under the seat in front of me, and pulled my shoulders inward to squeeze back into my seat. *This is really going to be a fun trip.*

The temperature inside the airplane cabin didn't help. I

reached up and opened my air vent. That made things feel a little better. I leaned back and sat, staring forward.

I didn't bring anything to read. What was I thinking? I should have stopped and picked up a novel in the airport. I never do that. It would have been kind of nice just to have something to escape into for a while.

I glanced through the seat pocket in front of me. *Maybe someone left a magazine in here.* But there wasn't much to choose from: a *SkyMall* catalog selling expensive gadgets that no one needed, instructions on using my seat as a flotation device in case we landed in the Mississippi River, and the monthly airline magazine. I opened the magazine and started reading an article about living on some Spanish coast. The houses were huge, the beaches white, the water crystal clear, the cliffs spectacular. *Who are they kidding? No real people live like this.*

Just then my cell phone rang. I squeezed forward, leaned down, searched through my bag, and caught it on the fourth ring. "Hello?"

"Hey, traveler. What's up?" It was my younger sister, Julie.

"Just got on the plane. Waiting to pull away from the gate."

"Did you get Sara taken care of, or do you need my help?"

"Well, theoretically she's taken care of. How Nick actually does with her, we'll see when I get back."

"What's he going to feed her?"

"He told me he's going to do some cooking."

I heard laughter on the other end. "Nick? Cook?"

"I know."

"Has he come back to earth, or is he still in the clouds?"

"Still in the clouds. He's totally flipped out on this Jesus thing."

"What are you going to do?"

"I'm not sure." I hesitated. "I called a lawyer yesterday and set up an appointment for next week."

"Mattie! You did?"

"I don't know. Maybe it's too soon. I just don't feel like I can take this anymore. I mean, things were already bad enough before Nick got religious. There's no way we're going to make it like this."

"I thought he'd been spending more time with you and Sara lately."

"Yeah. He has. I'm just not sure I want him to anymore. It's really confusing."

"Why don't you try counseling again?" she suggested. "Maybe a different therapist."

"What's the point? I mean, it's not like the last one did

much good. Besides, this is a different issue—not like Nick's workaholism. I just don't see any middle ground on this religion stuff."

I wanted to tell Julie more, but I heard an overhead announcement.

"I've gotta run," I told her. "They're telling us to shut off cell phones and all that. Can I call you tonight? I've got something else to tell you too."

"I don't know. I might be out."

"Julie, for once, don't go clubbing. It's bad news for you." One of the flight attendants walked by and gave me the eye.

"I'll call you tonight," I said. "Be there, okay?"

"Okay."

I clicked off the phone, put it in my bag, leaned back, and closed my eyes. *I can't believe Nick and I aren't even making it to our fourth anniversary.*

The plane taxied to the runway and took off.

two

"HAVE YOU CONSIDERED the possibility that your husband might be on the right track?"

The guy to my right, in the window seat, had folded up his *Wall Street Journal* and turned slightly to face me. He looked like the typical business traveler: thirty-five or so, wearing a blue suit, a light blue shirt, and a patterned red tie. He was average size, trim, with dark hair.

"I'm sorry?"

"I couldn't help but overhear some of your conversation. Has it occurred to you that your husband might be right?"

I looked at him incredulously. I couldn't believe this perfect stranger was butting into my personal business.

"Right about what?"

"About God. About Jesus."

"What do you mean?"

"Again, I wasn't meaning to eavesdrop, but it sounds like your husband may have found God."

You were eavesdropping, and you are starting to tick me off. "The only thing my husband has found is another excuse to go off and do his own thing. And excuse me for saying so, but this is none of your business."

I turned away from him and looked straight ahead. I could sense him doing the same. We both sat silently. *This is really uncomfortable. I've never had an incident with someone on a plane. I can't believe he had the gall to say anything at all.*

He lifted the paper out of his lap and held it toward me. "I noticed you were looking for something to read. Would you like to share my *Journal*?"

"No," I responded. "Thanks, though."

He put two of its sections back on his lap and opened the third. I flipped open my airline magazine once more. After a moment he lowered his paper. "Do you mind if I ask you another question?"

I used my finger to hold my place in my magazine while I closed it. "No, I guess not," I replied, trying to maintain a level of politeness. *I'm going to regret this, I know.*

"Have you ever thought about having a personal relationship with God?"

"No." I tried to respond without any emotion. "I'm not really into religion."

"I'm not talking about religion. I'm talking about a relationship."

"You're talking about God. That's religion."

"I'm talking about knowing God personally."

"Yeah, well." I opened the magazine again. "Whatever."

"Do you believe in God?" he asked.

"Not really." I buried my head a little deeper in the magazine. *I don't want to blow up at this guy.*

"So you don't think God exists at all?"

"Who knows? Look—"

"Let's assume that he does. Then we're talking about reality, not religion, aren't we?"

I looked up at him. "As I started to say, anything that has to do with God is religion. And I don't want anything to do with it."

He locked his fingers in front of him and stared at them for a moment before looking back at me. "Okay. Let me ask this. If you were to die tonight, do you know where you would go?"

"No!"

Two people in the row in front of me turned my way.

"No," I repeated. "I don't think I'll go anywhere. I don't know if I'll go anywhere. I'm not worried about life after death. I'm just trying to make it through this life." I held my magazine up to my face and shifted my body toward the aisle.

"I know," he persisted. "I just hate to see you throw your marriage away. I think if you—"

I slammed the magazine on my lap and turned toward him.

"Look, you don't know anything about me, my marriage, or my life. But here you are, trying to cram your beliefs down my throat. The last thing I need is more God talk. I was hoping to escape that on this trip."

"Why do you want to escape from part of your husband's life?" he asked.

"Because it's not part of who I am," I snapped back. "It's not part of who I want to be or what I want my family to be. If that's who Nick wants to be, fine, but he can do it without me."

I rose out of my seat. "Excuse me."

The man by the aisle got out of his seat and let me by.

The people behind us were staring at me. I walked to the back of the plane. Both bathrooms were occupied, and a woman appeared to be waiting for the next opening. I stood with my arms crossed, steaming.

I can't believe I was talking to that guy. I might as well have invited Nick along. I can't believe he would talk to me that way. I told him how I feel about religion. And then for him to say anything at all about my marriage!

A boy came out of one bathroom, and the woman entered.

Now what am I going to do? I can't stand back here the rest of the flight. But I certainly don't want to sit next to him again. I glanced at my watch. More than an hour and a half to Dallas.

I thought through my options. It was certainly too late to ask anyone to switch seats. I looked around for the flight attendants. Both were at the front of the plane starting to serve snacks and drinks. *I really need to get something into my stomach to settle it down.* A man came out of the other bathroom; I went in. *I guess I'll just go back and read. I can ignore him. Surely he won't say anything else.*

I returned to my seat as inconspicuously as possible. "Hey," the window-seat guy said as I sat down. "I'm sorry if I made you mad. I only—"

"Sure," I said matter-of-factly. "Let's just drop it."

"Okay. I hope the rest of your flight goes well."

"I'm sure it will."

I closed my eyes, and, mercifully, he shut up.

three

MY EYES HADN'T BEEN CLOSED two minutes when I heard a child's laughter. I opened them. A little boy, about four, kept ducking his head between the seats in the row in front of me and looking back toward the man on my left, in the aisle seat. His head would appear, and the boy would make a funny face, giggle, and hide behind his seat. The third time I glanced at the aisle-seat guy. He was making funny faces back.

The game went on for a few minutes until the boy popped his head over the back of his seat. He had a plastic fire truck in his hand. "You wanna play with my truck?" he said to the man.

"Sure. That's quite a fire truck you have there. How many fires have you put out with it?"

"I don't know. About a hundred."

The boy ran the truck over the top of his seat and down its backside as far as his arm would reach, all the while making truck noises. Suddenly he disappeared again, only to pop back up with another toy. "Do you want to play with my police car?"

"Absolutely," the man replied. The boy reached out with the car, and the man took it from him. They both ran the vehicles along the top and back of the boy's seat, emitting *vroom* sounds and pretending to almost run the car and truck into each other, then avoiding collisions at the last second.

"The doors and trunk open up," the boy stated.

"They do? Let me see." The man opened each one. "What do you put in the trunk?"

"Bad guys."

"Oh. Kind of stuffy in there, don't you think?"

"No. I let them out when we get to the police station."

They played a few more minutes until the flight attendants reached us with beverages and pretzels. *Of course, pretzels.* I requested cranapple juice. The man on my left asked for some orange juice. The window-seat guy missed his chance by dozing off, which was fine with me. The attendant put ice in a cup for me, handed me the cup, and held out the cranapple can. The aisle guy took it and handed it to me.

"Thanks," I said.

"You're welcome."

He opened his juice. I did the same with my can and poured it over the ice in my cup. I noticed that he wasn't using the armrest between us. *That's a first for a guy.* I staked claim to it by sliding my elbow over.

"Where are you heading?" he asked.

"Tucson."

"Business or pleasure?"

"Hopefully both. I'm going down to a new resort hotel to get a feel for the place…take a few pictures. I've heard they have a nice spa too."

"Are you a photographer?"

I laughed. "No, hardly. I'm a graphic artist. Well, part-time. The rest of the time I'm a mother."

"Sounds like you have a job and a half. At least."

"That's the truth."

We both sipped our drinks.

"You're pretty good with kids," I remarked.

"I love them."

"Do you have any?" The man was about my age, early thirties; maybe he had one or two small ones himself.

"No physical descendants, no."

I thought that was an odd way to describe kids.

"How many do you have?" he asked.

"Just one. A daughter. She's two."

"What a great age."

I smiled. "It is. She's already putting full sentences together. I have a feeling she's going to be a real chatterbox. Yesterday we were driving along, talking about birthdays, and she asked me, 'Mommy, could I have a dinosaur cake for my birthday?'"

He chuckled. "I love how kids are so drawn to dinosaurs. It's like they were made specifically for kids' imaginations."

"Sara's dad can't wait to take her to the natural history museum in Chicago. I figure that's more a boy thing, but it looks like Sara might enjoy it. In a few years."

I opened my pretzels and ate one. *Why do I ever eat these things?*

The aisle guy spoke again. "Sorry for your encounter with our friend next to you." He nodded toward the window seat.

"Oh, well. I'll survive. I guess I'm a little testy right now."

"I can understand why."

He sipped his juice and opened his own bag of pretzels. I assumed he was referring to my marriage. Everyone within five rows now knew I had a bad marriage.

"Have you ever been married?" I asked him.

"No, not precisely," he answered.

"Engaged?"

"I'm sort of engaged now, you might say."

"No date set?"

"Not one that we've announced."

Sort of engaged? With no date? What kind of engagement is that?

"Have you been together long?"

"It depends on your time frame, but, yes, quite a while."

I stuffed the rest of my pretzels into the seat pocket in front of me and took another drink. "You never know what'll happen in marriage, I suppose." I wasn't sure if I was talking to the man or to myself.

"How so?"

"Well, you know. People never expect to have marriage problems. I mean, everyone realizes they'll have some problems, but no one expects to…"

My voice trailed off. Here I'd been shouting at the guy on the right for getting too personal, and now I was on the verge of spilling my story to this man on my left. Granted, he seemed a lot less judgmental. Still, I didn't know if I wanted to get into the whole thing. After all, I didn't know him from…the guy by the window. But sometimes we feel more comfortable talking with strangers. That's why people pour out their hearts to bartenders, isn't it? They're safe. They'll listen to your story, avoid passing judgment, and comment if you want them to. At least, that's the theory.

I decided to continue with my train of thought. Or, rather, line of questioning. "Why do guys change after they get married?"

"What do you mean?"

"I mean…you've never been married, but you're a guy."

"You might say that."

"And you must have been in relationships before." *He's engaged and decent looking.*

"I've been in relationships forever."

Okay, not that good looking.

"So what is it with men? It's like they get you to marry them, and once they've caught the prize, their real self comes out."

"And women aren't that way?"

"Yeah, we are, but it's different. It's just…different. We don't totally change."

"Is that how it seemed with your husband?"

"Yes. Absolutely. I just wish Nick could be more like he was when I met him."

"What was he like?" Somehow he asked that as if he really cared about my answer.

"He had time for me. I mean, he was in graduate school then, so he was pretty busy, but he took lots of time out of his schedule for me. And when he was with me, he was really with me. Like, emotionally. Unlike now."

"How is he now?"

"After we got married, that all changed. We'd moved to Cincinnati, and he started working longer hours at his new job, and he didn't have time for me anymore. Or to do anything around the house, like at least pick up every once in a while or clean the bathroom every other weekend, which he used to do. I mean, we were together for three years before we got married. Lived together for two. You'd think you'd know someone by then."

I took a drink and sneaked a glance at the window guy. I was feeling a bit self-conscious. We were close enough to the engines that the people in the other rows couldn't hear me, but I certainly didn't want him eavesdropping on more of my personal life. He was still sleeping, though.

"I don't know," I continued. "I suppose marriage is a gamble that way. You can't be sure what course your partner's life will take. I guess the man you marry isn't really the man you marry. We carry a certain image of the person we choose, and we expect them to be like that after the wedding. But they aren't. At least, Nick wasn't."

"So what's brought things to a head?" he asked. "Something usually does."

I paused. This was going to sound pretty stupid. No, beyond stupid. "Well, a couple of weeks ago Nick came home late one night claiming that he'd had dinner with—I'm not kidding—Jesus Christ. Completely out of the blue. I mean, he seems to have been in his right mind one day, and then the next, he's making up bizarre stories and turning into a religious nut."

"So he's giving you the same story now…"

"Exactly the same. All he can talk about now is Jesus. He's never been religious before, not in the least. I've tried to ride this out, but it's driving me crazy."

"How have things been apart from that?"

"Actually, he's been around a little more. Spent more time with me and Sara. I think he finished a project at work. But I'd almost rather go back to the way we were. This is not the man I married. I didn't plan on religion making a sudden appearance. It's messing everything up."

"Religion always messes everything up," he replied. "I hate religion."

four

AT THIS POINT in the flight I experienced my second-worst nightmare of air travel (next to being trapped by an evangelist): the guy in front of me tilted his seat all the way back. *Jerk. Where do people get off thinking they have a right to put their seats back without asking? I'm five eleven! "Excuse me for making you miserable back there, lady, but I'm much more comfortable." Oh, no problem. Now I have the choice of either doing the same to the person in back of me or being transported to Dallas in a space half the size of my car trunk.* I resisted the urge to do what I always want to do, which is to nonchalantly dig my knees into the person's seat until they straighten back up.

I finally decided to put the issue out of my mind—my stewing wasn't affecting the guy in front of me in the least—

and get back to the man in the aisle seat. I wondered about his last comment, about religion. I had mixed feelings about delving further into it. I was already struggling enough with my feelings toward Nick's new diversion; I didn't know if I needed to egg them on. But I was curious as to his opinion.

"Why do you dislike religion?"

"Don't you?"

"Well…" Asked to provide an actual answer, I realized that wasn't so simple. I always said that people could believe whatever they wanted to and it didn't make any difference to me. Right now, though, I wanted to get as far away from religion as I could. "Maybe so. I'm not saying people don't have a right to believe what they want to. It's just not for me."

I poured the rest of my juice before resuming. "But what about you? You were the one who said you didn't like it."

"It keeps a lot of people from living life to the fullest," he answered. "It makes some people feel guilty over things they shouldn't feel guilty about and others worry about things they shouldn't worry about."

"I know! Religious people are so uptight."

He continued. "People spend their time doing things to placate some supposed deity. Unfortunately, it's wasted effort."

"You would think they would focus on feeding the poor or something."

"They often do. And that's a good thing. But so much of religion… People think that wearing special clothing or dipping themselves in a certain river or repeating specific religious phrases or abstaining from certain foods or traveling to specific sites earns them points. They do these kinds of things all over the world. American Christians have had their favorite rules: don't play cards, don't dance, don't go to movies—"

"Don't touch alcohol," I added. "We invited a few neighbors over one night for dessert, and one of the couples wouldn't touch the rum cake. Honestly, I was offended."

He laughed. "What's on the inside is what matters, not the external rituals."

"Totally," I agreed.

"Like the burka that some Muslim women are forced to wear."

"Is that the full covering that has slits for the eyes?"

"Right, the full covering. Most Muslim women want to dress modestly, and that's admirable. But many Muslim women are threatened or beaten for not having everything completely covered. That's evil. The men are afraid the women will make them lust. But you could put a woman in concrete blocks, and men would still lust."

I smiled. *I like this guy. He sees it like it is and tells it like it is too.*

"The problem," he continued, "is what's inside men's hearts, not what's on women's bodies. Controlling women is just an excuse for men to exercise their dominance."

"I despise that," I said. "And it seems like some people want to do the same things here! There's a church on our side of town that I heard doesn't even let women speak. I've felt like going there one Sunday morning and standing up in the middle of the service and giving them a piece of my mind."

He returned to the broader theme. "It angers me that religion has been used to justify such immense evil—slavery, racism, wars, oppression, discrimination. I hate that religion is the cause of so much ignorance and superstition in the world. I can't stand that religion is something people feel they have to escape from to lead normal lives."

"Yeah," I answered meekly as Nick popped back into my mind.

"Back where I grew up," he said, "religion and hypocrisy went hand in hand. I abhor people claiming to be one thing but in their hearts and actions being the exact opposite. I saw that all the time. The leaders just focused on the rules, which made them self-righteous. Then they would lay the rules on other people, who felt guilty when they couldn't keep them well enough. It was a big power play, a way for the leaders to keep themselves in positions of control."

"Where did you grow up?"

"In the East, in a small town."

"I've heard that small towns can be bad that way."

A flight attendant came by with a plastic bag for trash. I handed her my can but kept my cup, which had a little ice left. "Could I get some water?" I asked her.

"Of course," she said, her accent apparent. "I'll be right back with it."

In a moment she returned with a bottle of water and handed it to me. As she did, the aisle guy said something to her in a foreign language—maybe from Eastern Europe. Her face lit up, and she responded to him in kind. They conversed for a couple of minutes before she departed for the rear of the plane.

"You spoke that well," I commented. "What language was it?"

"Croatian."

"That's pretty obscure."

"I've spent some time there." He took the final sip of his

juice. "One of the things I dislike the most is when people who really do mean well get distorted by religion."

That was my biggest fear with Nick. Despite working too much, he really wasn't a bad guy. Until now, potentially.

"How do you mean?" I asked.

"People end up feeling they have to do certain things or be a certain way to be acceptable. So they stop being who they are, and instead they try to keep a bunch of rules that they can't keep, and all the time they feel guilty and miserable."

"It makes me miserable just thinking about it."

"Then they start distancing themselves from people they have meaningful relationships with. They're afraid that people who don't believe like they do will lead them astray. So instead of making them more loving, religion isolates them from the people they really do love."

I opened my water and took a long drink, then slowly screwed the cap back on. "I had a friend like that. My best friend in high school, Melinda. We had known each other since elementary school, but in high school we were on the volleyball team together, and we really got close. During our sophomore and junior years we did everything together. Then the summer before our senior year she became a Christian. Some church camp she went to."

"And after that?"

"After that our friendship was never the same. She started hanging around all her new Christian friends, and she did the Christian youth group thing, and she just didn't have much to do with me. I mean, we were still on the team together, and we still did some things, but it got less as the year went on. As a seventeen-year-old, I felt really left out."

"That's a shame," he said. "And it's exactly what I'm talking about."

"Yeah. I just knew we'd be friends forever. But I don't think we ever got together after graduation. I saw her at my ten-year reunion."

"What was she doing?"

"She had married some guy in college, and then they got divorced. I guess religion didn't help her much after all. No kids. She was dating some new guy at the time, and she was still doing her church stuff."

I unscrewed the cap of my water again and took another drink. He adjusted his body slightly to face me a little more.

"You're afraid your husband is going to do the same thing, aren't you? If not leave physically, at least emotionally."

I was surprised at his forwardness. "What are you, a counselor or something?"

"Actually, yes."

"Oh. I—"

"I didn't mean to be presumptuous. It just seemed like a similar situation."

"Yeah," I said, looking down toward my feet. "I got over Melinda after a while. High school friends, you never know. As for Nick…" I bit my upper lip to stop the tears that were welling up. "It's one thing to lose a girlfriend…"

I stared emptily for a moment. "First a workaholic, now a Jesus-aholic. Either way, Nick's not invested in me. What's the point of being married?"

"It doesn't sound like you really want to get a divorce."

"No." I surprised myself by how definite that sounded. "No, I don't. I want our family to stay together. But Nick is pulling it apart. Why is he doing that? Why did he try to get so close to me before we got married, but since the 'I do,' he doesn't really seem to care? I married to have a soul mate, not just to wear a ring and reheat dinners when Nick comes home late from work. Maybe most men grow distant like that."

He sighed. "A hard question. It depends on the guy. But mostly, men are afraid of being close. They weren't taught how to be close growing up. They weren't loved for who they are but instead for how they performed. They feel insecure and inadequate, and they don't want anyone to know them like they think they know themselves. They're afraid of being rejected."

"So instead they do the rejecting. Faultless logic that men have."

He shook his head slightly. "I wouldn't say they think through it on a logical basis at all. They naturally gravitate toward those things that make them feel competent and less susceptible to rejection, like work. They think these things will meet their soul's needs. They're wrong, but that's what they do."

"You're saying what they really need is intimacy, not work and sports and whatever."

"Work is important to a man. Very important. Providing for a family and feeling capable are part of who he is. But, yes, deep down, men want connection, just like women. They want to be loved for who they are, not what they produce. They want to feel accepted."

"So how does that relate to Nick's Jesus thing? I mean, this isn't the same as work is for him. He's not getting accolades for talking about Jesus."

"No, you're right," he answered. "This is completely

different. Nick's tapping into something deeper. If he listens well, he'll fulfill what his heart is really looking for."

"How is this going to give him what he's looking for?"

"That's the key question, isn't it? If you figure that out, you might save your marriage."

five

"*IF YOU FIGURE that out, you might save your marriage.*"

The man's words kept running through my head. Maybe he was right. Maybe my reaction to Nick's stuff was so knee-jerk that I hadn't taken the time to look beneath the surface. Not that I much wanted to, especially this particular surface. Couldn't it have been something else? Anything else?

Exploring why Nick was having an affair might have been easier. But if my marriage was going down the drain, the least I could do was try to understand it. I knew that the Jesus thing might just be a phase, but there had to be something underneath that had led him to embrace this stuff.

The little boy popped his head back over the seat. He was apparently heading to some beach, given the ensuing discussion with the man about sandcastles and moats and building defenses against the waves.

I picked up my airline magazine again and leafed through it. I glanced at an article on Texas wines that didn't interest me much. A couple of pages on Hilary Swank's acting career wasn't a lot better. *Why don't they ever have interesting articles in these things?* I guessed they didn't want to risk offending any fliers and had to water down their content to a bland lowest common denominator. I made another halfhearted attempt to find a piece that would grab my attention but failed. I put the magazine back in the seat pocket.

I looked out the window to see where we were. Down below, a patchwork of crops covered mostly flat land. That meant we were…somewhere between Ohio and Texas. A lot of good that did me. I glanced at my watch. *Thirty-five more minutes.*

I closed my eyes. Even though my body felt drained, I wasn't exactly tired. I just didn't have anything else to do. The man in the window seat started snoring lightly. That wasn't going to make the time pass more quickly. In front of me, I heard the boy's father offer him a snack. *Typical father. Has no clue about circumstances offering him a parenting break. If the kid was being entertained by the guy next to me, why divert him?*

I tried to purge my mind and relax, but it wouldn't purge. *"If you figure that out, you might save your marriage."* The thought kept pressing in on me. *I can either let events take their course, or I can try to be proactive about my marriage. I can try to figure out and relate to what's going on with Nick. Okay, maybe not relate to it but at least understand what's happening with him. If I can understand it, maybe I can do something about it.*

I felt a small sense of resolve awaken within me. *Things may be hopeless, but I don't have to let my marriage go down without a fight. I owe that to myself, and I owe it to Sara.*

I couldn't bring myself to think that I owed it to Nick. Given his performance as a husband, he owed me, big time. But at the moment, that wasn't the point.

Why would Nick suddenly turn religious? Nick's a bright guy. Why would he believe that stuff? Or need it? Nick isn't looking for a crutch in life.

I thought back over our relationship. Had Nick ever showed any sign of taking this direction? He had gone to church occasionally growing up, I remembered, but that was because his mother made him. He couldn't stand it and didn't believe any of it. He may have had a basic belief in God, but it was pretty minimal, and it didn't mean much to him. A couple of times Jehovah's Witnesses had come to our house. He virtually slammed the door in their faces. He ridiculed the church down the street and their transparent attempts to subtly proselytize the neighbors. He never showed the slightest interest in the New Age stuff some friends of ours had gotten into—except as something for us to laugh about together.

Nick was about as nonreligious as they come. He worked. And worked. And worked. And when he didn't work, he played golf, watched football, and listened to sports talk on the radio. God didn't appear anywhere on his radar screen.

It was like I woke up one morning and a new man was drinking coffee at the breakfast table. Did he decide that work wasn't doing it for him anymore? Actually, he had been working somewhat less lately. But why turn into a Jesus freak? I would have expected him instead to spend more time on the golf course.

The truth was, Nick's direction the last several weeks simply baffled me. It had come out of nowhere. It just didn't make any sense to me. Until I momentarily entertained one far-fetched possibility.

Maybe something did happen to him. No...that can't possibly be true. But overnight Nick went from being completely nonreligious to being a religious nut. He wouldn't have just decided on his own to do that one day. Would he? It doesn't fit him at all.

What happened to him? Is it possible that somehow he really did encounter God, or whoever? But what would that even mean?

I heard the familiar airplane *ding* and glanced up to see the seat-belt sign had come on. The flight attendant announced our final approach into Dallas. The window-seat guy woke up. I looked out over the city. The Dallas area had a lot more water around it than I had expected. And brown haze.

"A lot of pollution down there," I commented to no one in particular.

"The air has gotten terrible here," the window guy responded.

The man in front of me straightened his seat, allowing my legs to move again. His son had disappeared back behind his seat. I glanced over to the man on my left.

"I enjoyed talking," I said. "You gave me some food for thought."

He smiled. "I'm glad. I enjoyed our conversation too."

The plane landed and started taxiing to its gate. I sensed

the window guy leaning my way.

"You know," he said to both of us, "I overheard some of what you were saying about religion."

That's a shocker.

He continued. "I agree with some of what you said—the stupid stuff about religion. I mean, I go to movies, although not R-rated ones…well, except for *Saving Private Ryan,* which was great, and wasn't *The Passion of the Christ* rated R?"

The aisle guy answered for us. "Yes, it was."

"That was the bloodiest thing I ever saw. Have you ever seen so much blood?"

Neither of us responded.

"Anyway, people can get a little carried away with religious rules, but"—he was looking at the man on my left—"I think you're wrong when you say that religion stops people from enjoying life. In my experience, genuinely religious people—Christians, I mean—can enjoy life the most."

He looked back at me. "I'm not trying to be pushy. I simply think the two of you should consider that."

The plane stopped, everyone jumped out of their seats, and the noise level rose, effectively ending the conversation. *Hallelujah.*

Still seated, the man by the aisle leaned over and, in a

half whisper, said, "He means well."

"I doubt that," I responded.

We remained in our seats as everyone around us stood with the personal items they had rushed to retrieve. *Why do people always do that? It's not like they can go anywhere.* The plane finally cleared back to us. The aisle guy rose and stepped away from his seat. He didn't seem to have any belongings. He grabbed a suitcase from an overhead bin and set it down behind him.

"Isn't this yours?" he asked me.

"Thanks."

I took my suitcase and stepped into the aisle. As I was extending the handle, I heard him say, "Until next time." I looked as he turned and walked toward the exit.

"Yeah," I said, wondering what he meant.

It took a second for me to get my bag situated on top of my suitcase. I pulled it down the aisle, through the jet bridge, and into the terminal. I scanned left and right but couldn't see the guy in either direction. *Why am I even looking for him?*

I started walking toward my connecting gate. I passed all the airport staples: newsstands, gift shops, bookstores, food places. I popped into a bookstore. In the "Top 20 Bestsellers" area, I couldn't help noticing six religious books. I glanced around—*Who am I afraid is going to see me?*—before picking up one and leafing through it. I put it down and read the back cover of another. I returned it to the rack. *What are these things really going to tell me?*

I ambled over to the paperback fiction section and got a copy of Nicholas Sparks's latest novel (I had adored his book *A Walk to Remember*). I pulled my suitcase over to the cash register and placed my book on the counter.

"Just this, please."

The cashier placed the book inside a store bag and rang me up. I grabbed it and my own bag and balanced them atop my suitcase. I continued down the terminal and across a long walkway into the next. Just about the time I saw my gate in the distance, I passed a Starbucks. *Exactly what I want.* I had more than an hour until takeoff—plenty of time for a latte. I entered the Starbucks and got in line behind two men. The first ordered a Frappuccino. The second requested the coffee of the day and some coffeecake. The voice sounded familiar. He paid, then turned around. It was the aisle guy.

"Hi," he said.

"Hi," I replied. "Fancy meeting you here."

The cashier gave him his items, then motioned toward me. I stepped forward slightly. "Nonfat grande vanilla latte, please. Decaf." I was dying for the caffeine, but I wanted to be good. "And an apple-cinnamon scone." I handed her a ten.

I turned to the man from the plane. "You have a layover?"

"Yes. How about you?"

"Just over an hour left."

She gave me my scone, and we slowly moved toward the serving island. The employee making the drinks placed one at the hand-off point. "Nonfat decaf grande vanilla latte," he said. I reached for it.

The aisle guy grabbed a couple of napkins. "Care to join me at a table?"

"Sure."

He headed for the sole empty one, near the entrance. We sat and sampled our coffees. It felt a little awkward, accepting this invitation. I was still married, after all. *But what's the harm in having coffee with some guy I met on a plane? I won't see him again. And it's not like I was looking for him…exactly. Besides, he is a counselor.*

"So," he asked, "did you buy something at the bookstore?"

"How did you know I stopped at the bookstore?" I responded suspiciously.

"The bag you are carrying."

"Oh." I glanced over at it. "Yeah. I did. Nicholas Sparks. I've been wanting something good to read."

I took a bite of scone, then washed it down with some of

my latte. A question was forming in my mind. Given our previous conversation, I knew how he would answer. But I wanted to talk it through with someone, and this guy seemed safe, in more ways than one. And I valued his opinion. So…

"I was wondering…"

"Yes?"

"I was wondering, and I feel kind of stupid asking this, because of what we were talking about before…"

"Sincere questions aren't stupid."

"Well…" I couldn't make it sound any different than it did. "Do you think it's possible for someone to connect personally with God?"

six

IT WAS THE LAST QUESTION I ever expected to hear myself ask. I didn't even know if God existed. Now here I was asking this guy about personally connecting with God. He seemed to take it entirely in stride, however. Which is what I wanted, actually—someone with whom I could safely explore possibilities.

"Why do you ask?" he responded.

"Well," I answered, "given what we said before, about religion, you're probably going to think this is the dumbest thing you've ever heard. But after we talked, I started thinking about what's been happening with Nick. Him and his religious stuff, I mean. And as I thought about it, it still didn't make any sense to me. It doesn't at all fit who Nick is or what he would normally do. And, I don't know. I just got to thinking, maybe…maybe Nick really did have an encounter with God. Or Jesus. Or something." I paused for a second. "I know—that sounds pretty far-fetched."

"No, not really."

"But you don't even believe in God," I said.

"Your husband does, and he is the one focused on connecting with God. It seems to me, then, that it's worth your exploring."

I was surprised by his answer, but I was glad to have someone willing to talk it through. At least, I thought he was offering to talk about it.

"So do you think it's possible?" I asked. "Someone actually connecting with God?"

"What do you think?"

"Well, since I'm not sure there even is a God…"

"Are you saying that you don't believe in God or that you just don't know what to think about the possibility of God?"

I thought about that for a second. "I just don't know what to think about it, I guess."

"Then you think it's possible there is a God?"

"Well…it's possible, I suppose. I know, you probably think that's crazy."

"Why don't we assume that there is and go from there? Maybe we can figure out something about what Nick's going through."

That seemed like a reasonable way to explore the topic and maybe to discover some answers.

"Okay," I replied. "That seems good."

"So what if God does exist? Do you think it would be possible to connect with him?"

I answered honestly. "No, not really. I mean, God would be so much bigger and more powerful—so far beyond us, I guess—that I don't think we could presume to connect with him. What would be the basis for the connection? It would be like an ant trying to connect with us."

"That's a good question." He sipped his coffee. "What if you looked at it from the other side?"

"How do you mean?"

"I mean from God's viewpoint."

"What—could God relate to us?"

"No. Rather, would he want to?"

I considered that for a moment. "It's the same. I think the answer's the same. If there is a God, and he, or she, or whatever, is big enough to create the whole universe and all the time that's involved, billions of years, and here we are stuck out on this little planet in this nondescript galaxy—Nick always loves telling me about this astronomy stuff—anyway, what possible need would God have for us?"

"That's an extremely good question."

"I just have a hard time believing that any God would have much use for people, much less want to connect with them. I mean, wouldn't he have more important things to do?"

He laughed. "You might think that." He took a bite of his coffeecake and wiped his mouth with his napkin. "Maybe the answer to that question would lie in the nature of God."

"Meaning…"

"What would God be like? Would he just create everything, let it go, and watch it from a distance? Or, even further disconnected, would God be an impersonal force, like in *Star Wars*? Or would God be an involved being who thinks, chooses, and feels—who loves—like we do?"

I finished a sip of my latte. "Who knows? It's not like God makes a grand appearance to everyone. Who knows what God would be like?"

"Well"—he took a long drink—"work from the evidence you have. If there is a God, don't you think there would be clues as to what he is like?"

"Clues?" The cover of *The Da Vinci Code* suddenly popped into my brain. "What kind of clues?"

"What the universe would say about its Creator."

"Well, he'd have to be really old." I laughed.

"What?" he asked, grinning with me.

"I'm just picturing some really old guy who's kind of shriveled up and doesn't move around too well anymore, like they make actors look old in movies. God wouldn't be like that, I suppose. If you've been around for billions of years, you don't age, exactly."

He smiled. "No, I wouldn't think so." He had another sip of coffee. "So God would be really old. What else?"

"He'd have to be really smart. The universe is pretty intricate. And humans themselves are so complex, given what we've learned about DNA and all."

"Okay, God would have to be superintelligent."

"Yeah. I'm not sure I buy that design in the universe proves God, but if there was a God, he would be really intelligent—and powerful—to pull it all off."

"Why is that?"

"If we all got here by the Big Bang, then God would have had to fine-tune it to make the universe we have. I've heard Nick talk about how precise the whole thing is, how if just one of a thousand things were a little out of balance, the whole universe would be different, or we wouldn't be here at all."

I'm starting to sound like an advocate for the existence of God. But we are presuming that God exists…

"Okay," he said. "So if God exists, he would be really old, superintelligent, and very powerful—at least as powerful as the universe itself?"

"If he put it all into motion, then, yeah, I would say so."

"It sounds as though you're saying that whatever traits the creation has would reflect some greater trait in the Creator—age, intelligence, power."

I decided to think about that one for a minute. I didn't want anyone putting words into my mouth. I broke off a piece of my scone.

Could what he just said be true? Would the universe reflect the Creator? I suppose that's kind of a given. Whatever we make reflects us. Like my graphics. How could it be otherwise? What we create can only come out of who we are.

"All right," I answered. "That's a fair summary. I'm not saying I think it proves God."

"Understood." He had a bite of coffeecake. "So what if we bring this down to the level of people?"

"I'm not sure I'm following you."

"People are part of the universe. The highest native intelligence on earth. What would people tell us about God?"

"What do you think?" I asked. "I've been doing all the thinking here."

He laughed. "Okay, fine. I'll think a little too. I think that the various aspects of our being—our mind, our emotions, our capacity to choose, our conscience—would all reflect God. In other words, humanity's traits, just like the universe, would reflect the Creator. And the highest form of creation would most closely resemble who God is."

"Meaning people."

"Yes."

"But people can be awful to each other. You're not saying that's who God is too, are you?"

"That's a hard question, isn't it?" He sipped his coffee again. "Because evil exists. Is that part of who God would be, or instead has something gone wrong?"

"I don't know. If God was part evil, that would be pretty bleak. All I know is, the world is really screwed up, and lately it seems to be getting worse, not better. It's a little frightening to have children and not know when the next bomb will go off or something."

"I know," he replied. "It is frightening."

He had another piece of his coffeecake, and I had some more scone.

"You mentioned your daughter—Sara?"

"Yeah."

"Do you have a picture?"

"Of course."

I pulled my billfold out of my bag and held out Sara's picture to him. It was a really good one, with her new blue dress against a backdrop of red and yellow tulips at the arboretum. She had a pigtail sprouting out of each side of her head, and she did look precious.

"She's adorable," he commented.

"Thanks. We think so." I couldn't help smiling at the picture one last time before returning it to my bag.

"What do you do with her when you're working?" he asked.

"I take her to my cousin's three days a week. She has a three-year-old and a fourteen-month-old. Sara does great with them."

"How do you do being away from her like that?"

"I do okay. I really like my work, and I'm not sure how I'd do without a break from parenting sometimes. But some days I do have mixed feelings."

"Why is that?"

"It's just that when they're little, they do things every day that mean the world. Yesterday I had Sara at home, and we were talking about going to visit her grandmother and how Grandma was my mommy. Of course, she doesn't really understand how all that works yet, but she looked at me with those big round eyes and said, 'Mommy, I like you to be my mommy.' It just melts your heart."

He smiled broadly. "I bet it does."

I pointed a finger at him jokingly. "You just wait. One day if you have a little girl, she'll look at you like that, and you'll want to give her anything she asks for. It's worse for dads, I think. Nick would give Sara the world."

"Tell me," he said. "What do you like best about being a mom?"

I could feel a big grin slide over my face, and a joy washed over me just thinking about it. "Everything. You treasure the time they sit on your lap…feeling their soft hair, taking in their unique scent, being warmed by their little legs and back on you. Your own child is truly the most beautiful child in the world. You study her features more closely than any other person does. She comes from you, and she resembles you. You touch and hold her more than anyone else does, so you're able to absorb all there is about her in a unique way."

A smile had grown on his face as I spoke. "What else?"

"You love it when they discover something, like conquering the stairs or waving bye-bye. You love bragging about them to anyone. You could fill a book with how much you love them, how wonderful they are, and how they learn new things day after day."

I paused for a second, thinking about the things I treasured most about Sara and how I would go through all that again. "You know what else you love? You love the sound of their voice above all other kids'. It feels wonderful when Sara finds me and runs to me in a crowd of other kids and parents."

I thought about that morning at the breakfast table. "Though you can't always, you really want to give them what they want, like the sugary cereal or a stuffed animal—even if Sara already has more than I can count. You delight in the happiness it brings them, even if it's fleeting. And when they're naughty—which is often enough—you sometimes have to hold back your smile because they are so precious to you. Maybe that's what I like best: loving someone so much, regardless of what they do."

He leaned forward, put his elbows on the table, and intertwined his fingers. "Let me ask you this. If there was a God who created everything, don't you think it's possible that he would feel the same way about you that you feel about Sara? Love you as much? Want to give you the world? Want to be as connected to you as you are to her? In other words, is it possible that your love for Sara is a reflection of who the Creator is?"

I leaned away from the table and thought for a moment. "I don't know," I answered honestly. "I've never really considered that before."

He continued. "Do you think that people's desire to connect with God could have come from him? That God might have placed within them the desire for such a connection, because he is the one who actually wants it? That he designed them for intimacy with himself, and they are incomplete without it?"

"Maybe. I suppose it's possible."

"If this was the case, would Nick's course be a reasonable response to that God-placed desire? Would Nick's wanting a close connection with God be nonsense, or would it make the most sense?"

I sensed that we weren't dealing in hypotheticals any longer.

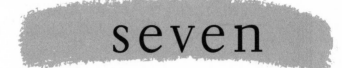

seven

"YOU SOUND LIKE you actually believe in God," I said tensely.

"I do."

"But…you said you didn't."

"Not at all. I said I hate religion."

"What's the difference?"

"Religion is what people mistakenly do to try to get to God—by being good enough, keeping certain rules, performing certain rituals, and so forth. But God? Of course I believe in him."

This was completely not what I was expecting.

"So you also think it's possible to know God personally?"

"Yes. I know it is."

I could feel my blood pressure rising. *This has all been a setup. He has the same agenda as Mr. Evangelism on the first flight, whose approach didn't work. So he pretended to be on my side. And I fell for the whole thing!*

"You're no better than that guy on the plane—no, worse! Here I am, pouring my heart out to you about my marriage, and all you want is to trap me into talking about God. At least the other guy was straightforward in his approach."

I reached for my latte and my bag.

"I wasn't trying to trick you," he replied. "I was simply helping you do what you said you wanted—to explore why Nick might be on this new course. I couldn't do that by stating up front my own perspective. You were too closed for that. But thinking through the issues and reaching your own conclusions—that's what you're trying to do, isn't it?"

Oh. Yeah. I am trying to do that, aren't I?

I folded my arms across my chest. "Okay," I conceded, "maybe I did say that."

I let myself calm down just a little. *But I'm still not happy with the subterfuge. Or with where this guy is coming from.*

I decided to give his motivation the benefit of the doubt and keep on conversing. *It's not that long before my next plane, so I won't have to endure much more if I get sick of it. And despite his religious beliefs, he is a counselor. Maybe he can actu-*

ally help. After all, how many counselors are willing to offer free advice during a trip?

I steered us back to my specific situation—Nick. "But not everyone's spiritual pursuit involves becoming so zealous as to claim to dine with Jesus. I mean, have you ever heard anyone say that?"

"It's been a while, I admit."

"Surely you're not saying that you think Nick really dined with Jesus."

"I think only you can decide whether to believe his story or not. I'm just trying to help you assess whether his direction of connecting with God is a reasonable one."

"And you think it is."

"Certainly. But I can't make up your mind for you. And I'm not the one who has to live your marriage."

"That's the truth." *Be thankful.*

I took another drink of my latte. "You said something a minute ago. You said that if God designed people for an intimate connection with himself, then we are incomplete without him. But don't you think that God is just a crutch for some people?"

"I suppose that depends on what you were created for," he answered. "If you were created for life without God, then he's a crutch. If, on the other hand, the very reason you were created is for an intimate relationship with God, then he's not a crutch. He's the fulfillment of what you were created to be."

"But you're implying that people can only be fulfilled through an intimate connection with God."

"Yes."

"But that's not true."

"Do you think people are truly satisfied in other things?"

"Of course. There are lots of people who are fulfilled who don't have God in their lives."

"Are you?"

"Well, no. But I'm not everybody."

"You are more everybody than you realize."

"I feel fulfilled in my career, for the most part."

"And as a parent," he added.

"Definitely as a parent."

"But not as a wife."

I could feel my eyes give a slight roll. "No. That doesn't rank quite as high on the fulfillment scale."

"Why not, do you think?"

"I don't know. I suppose I had this fantasy of what marriage would be like, starting with the wedding. Doesn't every woman have that? Well, we didn't make it through the ceremony without that fantasy going awry. I should have known we were in trouble when the minister, instead of saying that the rings represented an endless circle of love, said they represented an endless circus of love. It was his second wedding, and he was dyslexic, we were later told. I don't even know why we got married in a church. Anyway, he was right, after all."

"A lot of people start off on the wrong foot."

"Yeah, well, we never got on the right one. At least that's how it felt. That wasn't the case before we got married. Things were great then. But things are always great at the beginning of relationships. It's later I get bored. Except with Nick I really didn't. I stayed interested in him."

A large flight or two must have deplaned, because suddenly the ordering line had almost backed up to our table. We both shifted our chairs around to give people more room to stand, then picked up where we left off.

"What kept you interested in Nick, do you think?"

"I think it was because his whole world didn't revolve around me. He was real focused on his career, and I liked that."

"You don't seem to like it anymore."

"That's the truth. I suppose I got exactly what I wanted —someone who had another life, who wasn't too clingy. Now it's not enough."

"What would you say you want out of marriage?"

"I guess I want to be intimate in a way that's just as satisfying as the passion we first had. I know you can't sustain that level of passion forever; no one can. But I thought it would be replaced by an emotional closeness that would be just as good, in a sense. That hasn't happened, though."

I took a final sip of my latte, then continued. "Have you ever felt that way—a fulfilling emotional connection in a long-lasting relationship?"

"Yes, I feel that way all the time."

"You do?" I was taken aback by his answer. "How?"

"Well." He smiled. "That's kind of an involved story."

I glanced at my watch. *If we have time, I would kind of like to know his secret.*

He resumed. "What do you think stops you from experiencing that in your marriage?"

I pondered that for a moment. "I just don't feel completely known by Nick. He thinks he knows me, but he doesn't really understand what makes me tick, what my dreams really are, what... I don't know. For the longest time it was his work that kept him distant. And now, I suppose, it's this Jesus thing."

I felt myself straighten in my chair. "I do not plan on

being married to someone who lies in bed next to me watching a guy on TV touching people's foreheads, and then they fall down and pretend to be healed. I mean, who could stand that?"

He chuckled. "Is that what Nick watches?"

"No. Not yet. Or maybe he sneaks it in while I'm in the bathroom."

He laughed a little louder. I did too at the image of Nick flipping to those religious networks while I was brushing my teeth, as if they were the Playboy channel or something.

"So what if your marriage were more fulfilling?" he asked. "Would that satisfy you?"

"It would help."

"But would the deepest part of you be filled?"

"I don't know. It's just hard to imagine that with Nick."

"Would it have mattered if it had been someone else?"

"Well…maybe."

"Like who?"

"Like…" Only one person ever came to mind when I thought about this. "There was this guy I dated for a year in high school, Jason Payne. I was so head over heels about him. And ever since, I've wondered what might have happened if we had stayed together."

The ordering line had receded back to the counter. Nevertheless, I lowered my voice a little. "I think about him pretty often, actually. That sounds terrible, I know."

"It simply sounds like someone who isn't fulfilled. So what happened to the relationship?"

"He was a year ahead of me, and he was going to Stanford for college, and I started getting cold feet. I was afraid that he was going to meet someone there and that we wouldn't last, because I was going to stay in the Midwest for school. I didn't want to risk that rejection, and he had done a couple of things that annoyed me, so before he left, I broke up with him. It was the stupidest thing I ever did."

"You think you would have been happier with him?"

"Well…" I didn't like the sound of the truth. "Yeah. I do think that. That's not to say that I don't love Nick. Or didn't, anyway."

He leaned forward in his chair. "You know, you wouldn't have been any more fulfilled with Jason."

"How do you know?" *That's a pretty bold statement to make.*

"Because I know Jason."

"You do? Jason Payne? From Evanston? How do you know him?" I was trying to keep the excitement out of my voice.

"He met me after he moved to the Silicon Valley area. He's still there."

"Doing what? Is he married?" That sounded truly pathetic.

"He was. Twice."

"Twice? He's already been married two times?"

"Yes."

"What happened?"

"Both of them left him."

"They left *him*? Why would anyone do that?"

"Let's just say that he had his own issues. With which, I am happy to say, he is doing much better."

"Did you meet him professionally? I mean, in your counseling?"

"Not exactly. More of a personal relationship."

I sat back and stared forward. I couldn't believe it. Here I had entertained this fantasy for all these years: what if I hadn't broken up with Jason? And now, in the course of two minutes, that fantasy had been dashed to pieces.

"And, no," he said, "being with you instead wouldn't have helped him. He needed something more than a loving wife."

I hate how counselors sometimes know just what you are thinking.

"And marrying Jason," he added, "even with his having

worked through some of his issues, wouldn't have ultimately satisfied you, either."

"And why not?" *Dashing my fantasy is bad enough. You don't have to keep stomping on it.*

"Because people's souls are never filled up by human relationships. There is the initial thrill of romance and the chemical high that accompanies it, all of which is great. But that wears off. Eventually people settle into a relationship and find that it can't meet their heart's deepest longings. It wasn't meant to, so it's no surprise, really, that it doesn't."

"You're not saying that relationships are unimportant."

"No, not at all," he responded. "I'm just saying that true fulfillment can't be found in the created realm. Only God himself can satisfy the human heart. You were created for God. Nothing else will satisfy."

"But I don't believe that. I see happy people around all the time."

"How well do you truly know them, though? They may all be just like you: they have meaningful aspects of their lives, but ultimately they are not fulfilled. It's not that hard to put on a good face when you're around others."

"I just think lots of people are fulfilled—in their work, in relationships, in causes they devote themselves to. Plenty of things."

He looked at me for a moment. "Do you really think that? I don't think you do. Look at the society you live in. The list of things people try to fill themselves with is endless—alcohol, drugs, food, work, television, video games, sports, sex, shopping. I could go on. But nothing on this planet will satisfy the human soul."

"But not everyone is addicted or compulsive," I objected.

"No, some aren't. They seek fulfillment through parenting, balanced work, exercise, healthy relationships, social service. There are many positive things to devote yourself to. But these still don't fill the heart. When people get to the end of their lives—even those who have had good careers or marriages or parenting experiences—they're still not ultimately satisfied."

"How do you know?"

"Well, for one, many of them tell me. They won't tell anyone else, but when no one else is listening, they tell me."

"Why—because you're a counselor?"

"I suppose that has something to do with it."

"And what do they say?"

"That what they experienced wasn't enough. It may have been a good life, but deep down there is still some emptiness in their hearts."

"And you think that's because…"

"Because how is your heart going to be filled by someone, or something, as finite and imperfect as you are? If people were created to have an intimate connection with their Creator, would you expect them to be satisfied apart from him?"

He wiped his mouth with his napkin and set it on his pastry bag. "Maybe Nick has come to realize that, as important as you and Sara are to him—and I have no doubt you are—his heart was made for something more, for something transcendent, and he couldn't be fulfilled without it.

"And," he continued, "you're searching for something deeper too. Even if you don't know it yet."

"I'm just hoping for things to get a little better."

"That's the problem. Things don't usually get any better. Circumstantially, life is what it is. People hope things will improve, but they rarely do. Tomorrow will have its own set of frustrations and stresses and disappointments. Or things may get worse. You could lose your career. Or your family. Or your friends. Or your health."

"Sure," I replied, "those things could happen. But I can't base my life on that possibility."

He raised his eyebrows. "Possibility? Most of those things will happen. To everyone. There's only one thing that can't be taken away from you. When you find your fulfillment there, you can't ever lose it."

He unexpectedly stood up and pushed his seat under the table.

"We'd better go," he said.

"Why?"

"Our flight is boarding."

"Our?"

"You're going to Tucson, aren't you?"

eight

"BUT THE FLIGHT DOESN'T BOARD for another twenty minutes," I objected, looking at my watch.

"It's boarding now. Trust me."

"How do you know?"

"I just know. Can I carry your suitcase?"

I got up and placed my bag above my rolling suitcase. "No, I've got it."

We walked down to the gate, and, sure enough, they were calling my group. I got out my boarding pass and glanced at it. *An F seat. Next to the window. At least I'm not in the middle.*

The plane actually didn't look quite as crowded as the last one. Almost all the middle seats remained vacant as I walked down the plane to my row. I stopped. The counselor waited behind me while I put my suitcase overhead. I slid across two empty seats and got into mine before turning back to say farewell.

"Well, you've given me some food for thought," I said. "It was certainly an interesting conversation. What row are you on?"

"This one," he said as he sat down in the aisle seat on my row.

"This one?" I grabbed the boarding pass out of his hand and looked at it. *My row. Seat D.*

I handed it back to him. "Sorry. I was just surprised that we are on the same row again." He took the boarding pass and slipped it into his shirt pocket.

"Don't you think it's a strange coincidence," I asked, "our being next to each other two flights in a row?"

"No. Not really."

I put my bag in the seat between us. It didn't look like anyone would be sitting there. And it provided a kind of buffer in case the conversation took a turn I didn't want. Which it already had, I suppose. Here we were, talking about fulfillment in life and God and so forth, but somehow, with this man, I was more drawn in than turned off.

I was curious as to where he was heading right before we left Starbucks. But it did seem a little awkward, our getting on an entirely new flight, two strangers sitting next to each other again. And discussing the meaning of life. I thought maybe it was a good time to back up for a moment and at least get officially acquainted.

"I never did introduce myself," I said. "I'm Mattie." I reached across myself with my right hand.

He awkwardly bent his own hand around his armrest and shook mine. "Hi, Mattie. Call me Jay."

"Good to meet you, finally."

"You too," he said, smiling.

"Why are you headed to Tucson?" I asked.

"Business."

"What kind of business?"

"My father and I run a management operation, so to speak."

"Management of what?"

"Pretty much everything."

This guy is not real big on specifics.

"I thought you were a counselor."

"I am."

"You do that on the side?"

"No, it's part of the same operation."

I couldn't imagine what kind of operation that was, exactly, but I let it drop.

The plane's engines revved up. I looked out the window as we sped down the runway and took off. Once we were above the clouds, I turned back toward Jay. I figured we would resume our conversation where we had left off, but he had put his tray table down and was writing on a pad of paper. *Where did that come from? I didn't see him carrying anything.*

I watched him for a couple of moments, but he didn't look up. I decided to read my new book. It started quickly, as all Sparks's novels do.

The flight attendants arrived with drinks. I got another cranapple juice, which Jay handed to me. He got some water. And we both got the ubiquitous pretzels.

I opened mine—*Here I go, some more useless calories from a food I don't even like*—as he set his pretzels on the middle seat.

He started writing again. I opened my book and resumed reading. After a minute I set the book down and leaned slightly toward him. "What are you writing?"

"Oh, some favorite words of mine."

"Like what?"

"Poetry, mostly."

"Poetry?" I laughed a little. "You didn't say you were a poet."

"Someone else wrote it, actually."

"What are you trying to do, impress me?" I said half joking.

He smiled but didn't reply. To be honest, I was already impressed. I'd never met anybody quite like him.

"May I see some of it?"

He handed the pad to me. "It's free verse. At least it is in English."

I started reading.

I have loved you with a love that never ends.
Though the mountains be shaken
And the hills be removed,
Yet my unfailing love for you will not be shaken.

How could I give you up?
My heart is turned over within me.
I will take great delight in you,
I will quiet you with my love,
I will rejoice over you with singing.

"This is really good," I commented. "I mean, I love the intensity of feeling. Who wrote it?"

"My father did."

"You're kidding. What was the story behind it? What inspired him?"

"A relationship he had. One that he desperately wanted back."

I handed him his pad. He set it on the middle seat and opened his pretzels.

"God wants to love you with this kind of love," he said. "A passionate love."

"Passionate?" That was the last word I would have applied to God.

"God is pursuing you. He wants you to be connected with him forever."

I sipped my juice. "But I don't feel loved by God. Much less pursued by him."

"That's because you're so deadened to his voice. Everyone is at first. Humanity rejected God, and it's been deaf to him ever since."

"But that's too easy. To say we're all deaf to God—to me that just means God doesn't exist. If I say, 'Prove God to me,' and you say, 'Well, you're deaf to him; if you weren't, you'd hear him,' that's too convenient. It's just taking the facts and making up a story that fits them."

"Oh, people aren't entirely deaf to God," he replied. "They hear his voice in a variety of ways—just not nearly as clearly as they could if they were connected to him. It's like the difference between my listening to you and my listening to the captain when he came on a few minutes ago to tell us something about the flight, which was all garbled. Could you make out much of what he was saying?"

"No."

"People are like that toward God. They can hear him a little, but they can't make out much of what he's saying. When Sara was born and you held her in your arms and looked at her for the first time and you couldn't believe you could love anything so much, that was God speaking."

"That's exactly how I felt. I couldn't believe how much I could love this little person."

"When you stand above the California coast and look out to the Pacific Ocean, you feel so small. You know there has to be something greater than yourself in the world."

"I've experienced that."

"That's God speaking. When you fail to love Nick, and instead are angry and bitter and you retaliate, your guilt is God speaking through your conscience. You know that you weren't meant to live that way. It seems less than you were created to be, doesn't it?"

I shifted in my seat and looked out the window for a moment. I felt a tug toward what he was saying and a tug away from it. I turned back toward him. "Yeah, maybe. But it's almost impossible not to be resentful."

"I know it is. I'm just talking here about God speaking to your heart. All these things touch something deep within you because you were made for intimacy with God. He is the something bigger, the one who loves more than you could imagine, the one who forgives instead of being bitter. Connecting with him deeply is what your heart longs for. There is no being as delightful as he is."

Delightful? God? Delightful? I would have placed him more on the boring side of the spectrum.

As if reading my thoughts, he continued. "God is the least boring, the most fascinating, sublime, enchanting being that exists. How could he be otherwise? Delighting in God simply means that you derive your greatest joy and pleasure from him, because of who he is."

"Pleasure from God? You've got to be kidding."

"No, not in the least."

"How could anyone find pleasure in God? I mean, I can understand believing in God, but—"

"That's the statement of someone who's cut off from God. You don't realize how upside down what you just said is."

"What's that supposed to mean?" I replied somewhat defensively.

He had a drink of water and thought for a moment. "You know the hypothetical question, who would you want to have dinner with if you could dine with anyone from history?"

"Sure. I guess."

"What if you could dine with the one who carved the Grand Canyon, raised the Rocky Mountains, coded DNA, invented nuclear fusion, designed language, created the stars, establishes justice, fashions every newborn, and loves without end?"

"But God doesn't drop in on people for dinner."

He smiled. "Well, maybe. But what I am saying is this: God far surpasses any person or thing or experience this world could possibly offer. God is infinitely more delightful than anything or anyone he has made."

"But God—I mean, even if there is a God—reaching out to him... Who would know where to start?"

"You don't have to start," he answered. "God has already started. He is already reaching out to you. That's why he became a person."

"You know, if I could actually have dinner with Jesus, like Nick allegedly did, maybe I could believe too."

"Faith is a lot easier than you think. And you don't really need Jesus to show up. You do need to let go of what keeps you from trusting him and connecting with him."

"What's that?"

"You tell me."

I turned away and stared blankly out the window again. A swell of anger grew within me. I turned back his way and spoke measuredly, trying to keep my voice low enough so no one else would hear.

"Okay, I'll tell you what would keep me from trusting God and even wanting to connect with him. My younger sister was abused—sexually abused—by our uncle for six years, starting at age eight. I didn't even know for several years."

I paused to make sure I retained my composure. "Her life was ruined. And I couldn't stop it. I tried to, but I couldn't stop it."

I looked him straight in the eye. "I couldn't trust any God who would let that happen to her."

nine

HE RESPONDED slowly and quietly. "What you and your sister have endured is horrible. God hates it, just as you do. But how much of the world's evil would you like him to stop?"

"All of it!" I felt tears welling up in my eyes. "All of it! Can't he do that?"

"Yes, he could."

"Then why doesn't he?" I felt the first tears trickle down my cheeks. *Oh, great. I'm starting to blubber.* "I mean, look at my sister. Look at what that did to her. She starts sleeping around when she's in junior high. She gets pregnant. She drops out of school. She never trusts men. She's had two failed marriages with absolute jerks. She can't hold a decent job, she drinks too much, and she keeps looking for I-don't-know-what in these guys she takes home. Are you saying this was God's plan for her?"

I fumbled in my bag for a Kleenex, dabbed my eyes, then looked up at him. I saw something I never expected to see. His eyes were tearing up too.

"No," he said softly. "No. That is not God's ultimate plan for her. And it breaks my heart that she has had to go through all that. It breaks the Father's heart too."

Seeing his tears made mine return. "Then why didn't God stop it?"

"Mattie, there are no words I could say that would make sense, no reasons that would take away your pain. But I can tell you this. God is at work restoring people to their original design: to be connected to him, to be in a love relationship with him by their own choosing. One day the evil will be done away with, and all that will be left is good."

"But what about the people who do such evil in this world?"

"All things will be accounted for. The victims will be avenged, the perpetrators punished, the evil eradicated, the good rewarded. It's living during this not-yet time that's the tough part—knowing how terrible things are sometimes and how good they ought to be."

"I just don't understand why we have to wait."

"When humanity turned its back on God, it plunged itself into a world of great evil. Because of his love for people, God is at work making them into what he intended them to be. But he doesn't force them. That's the only way love can work. You have to choose to receive love, and you have to choose to give love. If you don't choose freely, it's not love."

"So is that it?" I asked, dabbing my eyes once more. "Are we just resigned to living with all this?"

"Recovering what humanity lost is a slow, person-by-person process. The human heart, once distanced from God, is not easily won back to its source of life and goodness. It seems like it would be, but it isn't."

"It just doesn't seem fair. My sister didn't ask to be abused."

"No, she didn't. It wasn't fair. It was horrible. God knows how horrible it was."

"I doubt that. I really doubt that. How could he know, sitting up there, or wherever, just watching?"

An expression of genuine hurt came over his face. "Is that what you think God does? Distance himself from the pain of people?"

"That's what it seems like."

"Humanity's rejection of God was incredibly painful for him. He had to watch his own children fall into darkness.

Can you imagine what it would be like to watch Sara's life spiral downward due to drugs?"

That image made me cringe on the inside. "Okay. So it was hard for God to watch us. But he doesn't do anything about it."

He shook his head. "No, you're wrong. He did the most that could be done. That guy on the first plane, the one talking to you about God—remember him?"

"How could I forget?"

"He didn't know you, so he didn't have the most sensitive approach—"

"You can say that again."

"But he did have some things right. He was right about the incredible suffering that God endured at the hands of humanity in his effort to win them back. You saw *The Passion of the Christ*."

"Which I regretted."

"The violence that Jesus endured only makes sense if you understand that here was God taking upon himself the punishment for the sins of humanity. He would do anything to be reconnected with those he loves—even die for them."

"Even if Jesus was God dying for humanity, what good did it do? Everything is still so screwed up on this planet. I mean, it's been two thousand years."

"What Jesus did was open a way back to God. He provided forgiveness—a clean slate—and the opportunity for people to be connected with God."

"But then what do you do? Once someone has connected with God, do they just sit around saying, 'Hey, now I'm connected to God!'?"

He laughed. "No. Not at all. Once you and God are joined to each other, you do what you do in any relationship: converse with him, get to know him, learn to delight in him."

"You mean you pray?"

"Yes. Although that word may not describe it well for you."

"But anyone can pray to God."

"Yes, but not everyone can hear him talk back. That's what a true relationship is all about. It's about deeply communing with another person. Once you establish a connection with God, he will teach you."

"Teach me what?"

"To listen."

"Do you think that's what Nick is doing?" I asked. "Learning to listen?"

"It's part of what he's doing—a crucial part."

"But what exactly does that involve—other than reading the Bible, which Nick has been doing lately. Anyone can do that."

"Yes, but not everyone can hear God speaking to them through it like Nick now can."

I was taken aback by his statement. "What? What makes Nick so special?" *He is my husband, and he is talented, but he doesn't seem that extraordinary to me.*

"What makes Nick so special is that he is no longer the person he used to be. God has given him a new spirit."

"But what's the difference between that and just becoming religious? It's the same thing."

A baby was crying a number of rows back. I turned that direction. It might have been crying for a while; I'd been pretty wrapped up in our conversation. Three years before, the sound would have driven me crazy, but with a two-year-old of my own now, I had a lot more patience. The mother stood up and walked the baby toward the rear of the plane. I turned back to Jay.

He resumed. "It's not the same thing at all. Just the opposite. Becoming religious is about outward things mostly. Do this. Don't do that. Go here. Avoid going there. I'm talking about someone becoming new from the inside out. When you put your trust in Jesus, God gives you a brand-new spirit, a clean one."

"You mean, like a new attitude?"

"No, an actual new human spirit. The old one was dead

to God. It couldn't connect with him. You have to have a new one, one that's alive to God. He then comes to live in you, and he connects with you on the deepest possible level—a level where you can hear him."

"So you're saying Nick is experiencing this now?"

"Yes."

"What does that mean exactly? Nick isn't hearing an audible voice from God, is he?"

"No, of course not. He doesn't need to. God's Spirit can communicate directly with Nick. Usually the Spirit does that through God's written word."

"The Bible?"

"Yes."

"So what if someone does establish this connection with God? What does God have to say to them?"

"The things I wrote before, for one."

"The poetry? I thought you said your father wrote that."

"God is my father."

That sounded a little strange, but I let it pass. "Those things were from the Bible?" I asked.

"Yes."

"But I've always thought of the Bible as mostly a rule book…how to be a good person, you know."

"Then you've missed its message entirely."

He reached for his pen and wrote some more as I watched. When he finished, he handed the pad to me. "Does this sound like a rule book?"

I read what he had written.

Therefore I am now going to allure you;
I will lead you into the desert
And speak tenderly to you.

I have engraved you on the palms of my hands.
As the bridegroom rejoices over his bride,
So I rejoice over you.
Therefore my heart yearns for you.
One day, you will call me "my husband."
I will betroth you to me forever;
I will betroth you to me in love.

I have made myself one spirit with you.
I nourish you; I cherish you.
I give myself up for you.
I lay down my life for you.

I looked up at him. "The Bible says these things?"

"Yes. God wants to say them to you. He wants to say

them when you read his word. He wants to whisper them to you as you go through your day. When you stop to be quiet and listen, he wants to say these things, and so much more, to your heart. That's the way Jesus lived on earth. He listened to his father's voice."

"So are you saying that Christianity is just sitting around quietly and listening?"

"No, hardly. Life with the God who loves you is many things. Loving God and loving others, when you boil it down. But no one can do that adequately. Only God can. That's why he joins himself to people, to live his supernatural life through them. A life of love is simply the outflow of God through a person."

"And that comes through listening?"

"In large part. Your heart is changed by deeply knowing God's heart toward you. Hearing how you are loved. Hearing how you are forgiven. Hearing how you are accepted and delighted in and how you have a special place in God's family. What if you lived in a place where these were the constant messages you received?"

"That would be a nice place."

"And it's available to you now. You can find that place in Jesus Christ, through faith in him."

I thought about the messages that I did consume—

about needing to be the perfect mom, the perfect wife, the successful professional, the woman who could keep up with models who were always younger, prettier, skinnier. Who could measure up to all of it?

He continued. "What God wants to say to you is something you need to hear from him every day, just as Sara needs to hear from you and be shown every day that you love her."

I thought about Sara. Then for some reason my sister popped back into my mind. "What about Julie?" I asked somberly. "She hasn't experienced much of God's love."

"That doesn't mean God hasn't loved her. I can tell you this: in the midst of all her pain, your sister will choose to be reconnected with God. She will know his love deeply. And there will come a day when God will personally wipe away every tear from her eyes. She'll never hurt again. And the hurt she did experience here will seem as nothing to her then, for she will have God."

"But she's having to go through so much now. And I hurt so much for her."

"You know what? She hurts for you, the things you are having to go through. The issue isn't whether we've experienced pain. All people have, even those who seem to have it all together. God is bigger than people's pain, and he can heal it. God's·love heals all."

I sat back, somewhat stunned. "This isn't at all what I understood Christianity to be."

"It's what you were designed for: to be joined to God, to know his love, to relate to him intimately."

I certainly didn't want to commit myself to anything, but I couldn't help but ask the logical question. "So what do I do with this?"

"You have to answer this: do you want to be joined to perfect love?"

ten

A FLIGHT ATTENDANT came on the overhead speaker and announced that we were starting our descent into Tucson. Jay put his tray table up. I noticed that he hadn't reclined his seat.

I sat quietly in my thoughts for a moment. *I can't believe what I'm considering. I got on this plane, avoiding God and ready to divorce Nick, and now... But do I have to go down this path to...*

I waited for Jay to turn to me before I spoke. "Are you implying that I have to go down the same path as Nick to save my marriage?"

"No."

"But it seems like it. Here Nick is going off in his own

direction, and I just feel like he's getting farther away from me."

"That depends on what you mean," he said. "Nick is getting farther away from trying to find fulfillment in life without God. So if that is your common ground, you're right."

That doesn't sound particularly hopeful.

He continued. "But in a very real sense, Nick is moving closer to you. He is growing in his ability to truly know you and truly love you. That's what you want in your marriage, isn't it—to be known and loved?"

"Yeah. That would be nice."

"And Nick is learning to do that better. Of course, he won't ever do it perfectly. He can't fill the deepest parts of your soul. Only God can."

Maybe so. But I still wish I had more of that from Nick. "You say Nick is changing, learning to love better. How—" *I don't know any way not to make this sound self-centered.* "How is that going to happen? Because I'm not going to feel all that loved if Nick just sits around all day reading his Bible and listening to God."

"Is he doing that now?"

"Well, no."

Actually, despite my adverse reaction to Nick's God thing, I couldn't deny that he had been a better husband the last number of weeks. Not that I gave him much credit for it, but he had been more attentive, a little less selfish, and certainly more emotionally present. *And he is taking some time off to take care of a two-year-old, which really is a miracle.*

"Learning to love well takes time," Jay said, "because it means laying down our selfish interests and living for the sake of another. That's a major shift. So you can't put a timetable on it. It's not like learning in a classroom."

"But…" *This is going to sound petty.* "It annoys me when Nick gets up at six o'clock now on Wednesdays. He has this men's group that he's started to go to. It's kind of a Bible study, I guess. I don't know. It's just so unlike Nick."

He laughed. "You don't expect Nick to teach himself, do you? Has it occurred to you that maybe these guys will actually help Nick learn to experience God deeply and so love you better?"

"That's the last thing that would have occurred to me."

"You know, you haven't realized it, but Nick's side of this marriage is taking care of itself. He will end up being a better husband than you ever thought he could be. The question now is, will you start growing into the kind of wife you could be? The only way you can do that is to have God himself living in you and to learn to hear his voice."

I hadn't been paying attention to our flight, and I was

startled when the plane landed with a jolt. We taxied briefly. I sat, thinking.

We stopped at the gate. As usual, everyone rose. A Hispanic couple with a child and an infant stood up across the aisle from us. The mother looked toward the bin above us.

Jay stood up and said something to her in fluent Spanish. She smiled, pointed at the bin, and said something in reply. Jay reached overhead and pulled out two small suitcases and set them in the aisle.

He turned back toward me.

I stood as well. "How many languages do you speak?"

"All of them."

"What do you mean, all of them?"

"I mean all of them."

"All the languages there are?"

"Yes."

"Say something in Mandarin for me."

He spoke in what sounded like Chinese. I wasn't sure what to say. "No one can know every language. There are thousands of them."

"I can."

I just stared at him.

"I've had a lot of time to practice, so to speak."

The aisle had cleared almost to our row. Jay leaned toward me. "We were talking about listening to God."

"Uh-huh."

"Would you like to practice a little?"

"Sure, I suppose." I had no idea where this was going.

He half whispered just above the noise of the passengers. "When your sister, Julie, has a baby boy one day, tell her not to worry about clothing. She can borrow yours."

"But I have a girl."

"I know. But starting in January, you'll have plenty of boy clothes. Congratulations, by the way." He smiled broadly, turned into the aisle, and walked off the plane.

I stood, motionless and speechless. *I haven't told anyone that—not even Nick.*

After a few seconds I snapped out of my daze. I gathered my things as quickly as I could. Three people went by in the aisle before I finally cut in front of someone, virtually knocking her out of the way. *Sorry. I have someone to catch.* I rushed down the aisle, pulling my suitcase behind me, then darted past a group of people in the jet bridge leading into the terminal.

"Sorry. Sorry!"

I burst into the terminal and looked to the right, then to

the left, then straight ahead. *No one.* I looked in every direction again. *Nothing.*

I glanced at the signs above me. Ground transportation was to the right. I ran past the gates and the shops and all the people waiting for their next destination. My eyes scanned to and fro while my brain processed clues from the last few hours.

And then it hit me—what had been right before my eyes the whole time.

I bolted toward the end of the terminal. Seeing an information counter, I veered over.

"Where are the hotel vans?" I asked, out of breath. *He'll be at the shuttle pickup,* I reassured myself.

The man pointed me to a waiting area outside. Pulling my suitcase, I ran out, dodged two cars dropping off people, and arrived at the shuttle lane. The bench there was empty. I looked to my left. A couple of lanes over and a little way down, I saw a familiar face. A taxi was slowing to pick him up.

I left my luggage behind as I sprinted toward the taxi. "Wait!" I cried out. "Wait!"

The man spoke to the taxi driver through the passenger-side window for a moment, then turned toward me as I approached the cab. But he was a stranger.

"Oh," I said, "I'm sorry. I thought you were a friend of mine."

"No problem." He opened the cab's door and slid inside.

I walked back toward my luggage. *Why couldn't that have been him? Did he just disappear?* I looked to my right, through the glass doors into the terminal. Nothing. The thought crossed my mind that maybe I should check baggage claim. *But he didn't have a thing with him. He probably didn't have any luggage at all. Why would he need luggage?*

I heard a vehicle approaching. I glanced back over my shoulder and saw my shuttle. I picked up my pace, but the shuttle got to the bench before I did.

"Hold on a sec!" I shouted as I got within range.

The shuttle driver appeared from behind the van and walked over to my luggage. I noticed his dreadlocks as he reached for the suitcase.

"Do you want the little bag with you or in the back?"

His accent sounded Jamaican. *Or at least what Jamaican is supposed to sound like.*

"I'll keep it, thanks."

He put my suitcase in the back of the van. I looked inside the front. It was empty. I sat in the row behind the driver's seat. The Jamaican took his seat and shifted into drive.

"Could you wait here for just a minute?" I asked. "Somebody else might join us."

"Sure thing," the driver answered. He glanced at me in the rearview mirror. I looked out the window, hoping to see Jay's face. *He even called himself Jay. How could I be so blind?*

The driver started humming a tune. A minute passed. He straightened slightly. "Ready to go, or should I wait a little longer?"

I took one last look around, then fighting off a pang of disappointment, said, "You can go."

The van pulled out and started toward the airport exit. The driver turned on some reggae music. I pondered.

Why did he leave like that? At least Nick got to figure out who he was and ask him some questions. Why did he wait until the end to make his identity obvious?

And why did he appear to me at all? Or to Nick? It's not like we're something special. Does he connect with people all the time?

As I thought it over, I felt astounded by the encounter and let down all at the same time. *Now what? What do you do after this kind of experience? Would anything else on earth come close?* My mind raced, running through the conversation we'd had.

We arrived at the resort. I checked in and made my way to my room—quite a hike, given the size of the place. I tried scoping out the place a little during my walk, but work was the last thing on my mind.

My room was spacious and elegant. *As I expected.* I parked my suitcase at the foot of the bed and freshened up a bit in the bathroom. I walked back into the bedroom and sat on the bed. I looked over at the phone and noticed a box covered with wrapping paper. I picked it up. On the top, tucked under the ribbon, was a small card with "Mattie" written on it. It wasn't Nick's handwriting.

I unwrapped the box first and looked inside. The present was wrapped in tissue paper. I pulled aside the paper and held up a darling blue newborn outfit. A white sheep decorated the front.

I reached for the envelope and pulled out the card. I opened it and read the words handwritten on the inside:

> My sheep hear my voice,
> and I know them,
> and they follow me;
> and I give eternal life to them.

Readers Guide

1. What do you see as the primary theme of *A Day with a Perfect Stranger*? In what ways does this theme relate to your own life? Explain.

2. What aspect of the book held the most meaning for you personally? Why?

3. What in the character of Jesus, as presented in the book, appealed to you the most? Why?

4. What would you say is the main purpose of Mattie's life before she encounters Jesus? What life purpose does Jesus invite her into?

5. Why does Mattie find her marriage unfulfilling? Can you relate in any way to the hopelessness Mattie feels about her relationship with Nick? Perhaps in your case it is a relationship, or perhaps something else. What is the hope that Jesus offers her? How does that hope relate to your situation?

6. How does Jesus use the word "religion" in the book (see page 57)? What does he say religion produces (see especially chapter 4)? In what ways has religiosity pushed you further away from real intimacy with God?

7. Jesus comments that people (men in this case) often "weren't loved for who they are but instead for how they performed" (pages 32–33). Where can you find love that is

unconditional, rather than based on how you perform? How could knowing you are loved that way affect your life?

8. Talk about Jesus's and Mattie's discussion of fulfillment in life. From what things have you personally sought fulfillment? How much fulfillment did these things end up providing? Explain.

9. If your life continues in its current direction, when it draws to a close, will you have been ultimately fulfilled? Why or why not? What implications does this have for decisions you may want to make?

10. On page 66, Jesus says, "True fulfillment can't be found in the created realm. Only God himself can satisfy the human heart. You were created for God. Nothing else will satisfy." What implication does this have for how you are living your life?

11. Can you relate to how Mattie describes parenthood (pages 52–54)? If you are a parent, what does your love for your children tell you about God's love for you?

12. Read back through the Bible verses Jesus writes on the pad (pages 75 and 88). Based on these verses, how would you describe God's heart toward you?

13. Between you and God, who is really pursuing whom? What are the implications of the fact that you are a responder in a relationship with God, not an initiator?

14. On page 83, Jesus says, "The human heart, once distanced from God, is not easily won back to its source of life and goodness." Why do you think this is the case?

What is blocking you from fully experiencing the source of true life?

15. Jesus speaks to Mattie about the importance of listening to God. To listen, one must be connected to him at the deepest level. How does Jesus indicate this connection is established (see the bottom of page 89). Have you made this permanent connection?

16. What does it take to really listen to someone? What might it take to really listen to what God wants to say to you?

17. In the book, what does Jesus mean when he talks about delighting in God (see pages 78–79)? What would it look like for you to delight in God? How would it change your life if you did?

18. Think about Jesus's and Mattie's conversation about her sister, Julie, and suffering (pages 81–84). For Julie, why will having God overshadow the pain she has experienced? In what way can God's love heal all?

19. Think about suffering that you have experienced in your life. How do the following facts affect your perspective on suffering?
    • God himself suffered more than anyone by dying for your sins.
    • God uses your suffering to awaken your need for true intimacy with him.

20. Why would having God live in her, learning to listen to God's voice, and deeply knowing God's love enable Mattie to become the person she was meant to be?

About the Author

DAVID GREGORY is the best-selling author of *Dinner with a Perfect Stranger, The Next Level, The Last Christian,* and the coauthor of the nonfiction book, *The Rest of the Gospel.* After a ten-year business career, he returned to school to study religion, sociology and communications. He holds master's degrees from Dallas Theological Seminary and the University of North Texas. A native of Texas, he now lives in the Pacific Northwest.

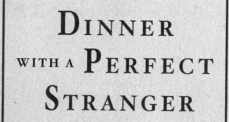